# A Christmas Surprise for Chabelita

written by
## Argentina Palacios

illustrated by
## Lori Lohstoeter

Troll Medallion

Library of Congress Cataloging-in-Publication Data

Palacios, Argentina.
A Christmas surprise for Chabelita/by Argentina Palacios:
pictures by Lori Lohstoeter.
p.  cm.
ISBN 0-8167-3131-4 (lib.)    ISBN 0-8167-3132-2 (pbk.)
[1. Mothers and daughters—Fiction. 2. Grandparents—Fiction.
3. Panama—Fiction.]
I. Lohstoeter, Lori, ill. II. Title.
PZ7.P1753Ch 1993 [E]-dc20 93-22336

To my mother, Jilma George, who taught me the poem *"Caperucita Roja,"*
and to the memory of my grandparents, Santos George and Adela de George,
who taught me many things.— A. P.

For Ashley, the inspiration for the sunshine in my paintings.— L. L.

When Chabelita was a little girl, her mother went away. She went to teach in a big city.

"I want to go with you," Chabelita cried.

"No, honey. There won't be anyone home to look after you. For now, you must stay with your grandparents. *Abuelita* and *abuelito* love you very much," her mother said.

Chabelita was sad.

"Look, Chabelita," her mother said, pointing to a map. "Here's where we live, and here's where I am going. It's not so very far away. I will try to come home on weekends and holidays. And, I will be here for the entire summer.

"I will write often," said Chabelita's mother when she left. "I will send you gifts, too, you'll see."

Chabelita's grandparents lived in a big house, just the two of them. Their own children were grown. They had families of their own. They lived in other places.

Grandma and Grandpa were happy to have Chabelita for company.

Chabelita and Grandpa were best friends. They went to market together every morning. They bought the food for the day, each day. Grandma gave them a list of what she wanted.

"When you buy food one day at a time, everything is always fresh," Grandma said.

Grandpa enjoyed going to the market every day. He could see his friends and chat with them for a while.

Chabelita liked going to the market, too. There were so many fruits and vegetables of all colors. She didn't like the butcher section, though.

Sometimes, Grandpa and Chabelita went to the river bank. The people from the country, the *campesinos*, brought fruit and vegetables to sell in the market. Some brought the produce on horseback. Some came on a raft. Others carried the food on their backs.

"How much for the oranges?" Grandpa asked.

"For you, Don Ernesto, 100 for 50 cents," a man said.

Grandpa often bought a sack of 100 oranges.

Grandpa and Chabelita also walked to the post office.

"*Buenos días, Don Ernesto. Buenos días, Chabelita,*" the people said along the way.

Don Ernesto and Chabelita answered everybody's greetings.

"*Señorita*, is there any mail for me, or for my granddaughter?" Grandpa asked at the post office window.

"Yes, there is, Don Ernesto. A letter for you, and a package for Chabelita," said the clerk.

Chabelita was very excited with her package. She started to open it right there in front of everyone.

"*Niña*, you must wait," Grandpa said. "It is not proper to open a package in public."

"Let's go home quickly, *abuelito*. I want to see what's in the package," said Chabelita.

"Look, *abuelita, mamá* sent me a package!" Chabelita exclaimed.

"Open it carefully," Grandma said, "so you don't damage what's inside."

"Ah, a red dress! And a pair of shiny black shoes! How beautiful!"

Chabelita loved the red dress and the shiny black shoes. She loved them so much she wanted to wear them all the time.

Grandma said, "That dress and those shoes are too good to wear every day. We will save them for special occasions."

On the first day of school, Grandma told Chabelita, "This is a special occasion. You may wear your red dress and your shiny black shoes if you wish."

"*Gracias, abuelita*," Chabelita said.

Chabelita also wore her special shoulder bag that day.

She felt very grown up.

Grandpa walked with her to school.

Grandpa now went to the market and ran his errands all alone. He missed Chabelita. His friends missed her, too.

They asked Grandpa, "Where is Chabelita? Is she sick?"

"Chabelita is in school now," he said.

Chabelita loved school. Since she had no brothers and sisters at home, she loved to play with the children at school.

School was fun.

When Chabelita's mother came home one weekend, she taught Chabelita a poem. It was called *"Caperucita Roja."* It was a poem about Little Red Riding Hood in Spanish.

"You know, Chabelita," said Grandma, "'Little Red Riding Hood' was your mother's favorite story when she was your age."

The poem was long, but it was very beautiful. Chabelita memorized it and recited it in school.

A few weeks later, when Grandpa came to meet Chabelita after school, the teacher spoke to him.

"Don Ernesto," she said, "the school is going to put on a holiday program. It will be the week before Christmas vacation. The whole town is invited. We would like Chabelita to recite '*Caperucita Roja*.'"

"Yes, yes, yes," said Chabelita. "I can do it."

As the night of the program grew near, Chabelita was excited. But she was also a bit nervous.

"I am one of the youngest in the program," she said to Grandpa.

Then she whispered to Grandma, "I wish *mamá* were here."

"Don't worry, Chabelita," said Grandma. "I know you'll do your best. Grandpa and I will be proud of you. Other people will be proud of you, too. You never know who might be watching."

The night of the performance, Chabelita recited the poem. And, she didn't forget one single line.

Everybody applauded. Then she bowed.

Chabelita was done.  Now she went to sit with Grandma and Grandpa in the audience.

Half-hidden behind them, a lady held a big bouquet of red carnations.  Chabelita stared at her.  She couldn't believe her eyes.

"*Clavelitos rojos para mi Caperucita Roja,*" said her mother.  "Red carnations for my Little Red Riding Hood."

"We told *mamá* about your performance," said Grandpa. "It was hard for her to get away, but she didn't want to miss this for anything!"

"We wanted to surprise you," added Grandma. "It's an early Christmas present." Then Grandma and Grandpa smiled at Chabelita. "For both of you from both of us!" they said.

## A NOTE ABOUT THE AUTHOR

Argentina Palacios was born in Panama, where the story of Chabelita is set.  In fact, the author's own childhood was very much like Chabelita's.  She, too, was raised by loving grandparents after her mother went to teach in another city.  And she, too, learned a poem called, *"Caperucita Roja,"* which tells the story of Little Red Riding Hood.

*"Caperucita Roja"* was written by Gabriela Mistral, a Chilean author who won the Nobel Prize for Literature in 1945.  To this day, she is the only Spanish-speaking woman ever to have won that honor.